The Penguin and the Fine-Looking Fish

Written and Illustrated by

Cindy R. Lee

Cindy R. Lee, LCSW, LADC
PO Box 14060
Oklahoma City, OK 73113

The "with respect" concept as it relates to "children from hard places" was derived from the Trust-Based Relational Intervention ® resources (Purvis & Cross, 1999-2015.) For more information, please read Purvis, K.B., Cross, D.R. & Sunshine, W.L. (2007) *The Connected Child: Bringing Hope and Healing to Your Adoptive Family.* New York: McGraw- Hill.

Cassidy, Jude. "Truth, Lies and Intimacy: An Attachment Perspective." *Attachment and Human Development, Vol 3 No2.* 2 September 2001: 121-155. Print.

Acknowledgements:
Thank you to Christopher, Amanda and Jack for all your advice, input and support. Mutte, Christie, Eric, Zachary and Emily are all wonderful supporters. Special thanks to Kelly and Amy Gray, David and Jean McLaughlin and the McLaughlin Family Foundation for giving the gift of healing to foster and adopted children. Thank you to Casey Call, Henry Milton, Brooke Hayes and Jennifer Abney for all their support and guidance. Gratitude also goes to Cheryl Devoe for donating her time and editing skills to this project.

Bless you to all of you who have opened up your homes to foster and adopted children and bless you to those of you who support all those who do.

For Jack and his
love of penguins.

How to Show Respect

Teaching Tips for Parents by Cindy R. Lee, LCSW

R-E-S-P-E-C-T! Humans show this trait when engaging in meaningful connections with others throughout our lives. Driven by love, we strive daily to be respectful and to teach our children to be respectful. We teach proper table manners, the importance of sharing, the value of cleanliness, and the need to say please and thank you. We model respect as we teach these skills by offering praise and playfulness to validate the dignity and worth of our children. As a society, we value respect because we believe we are worthy of love and others are worthy of love.

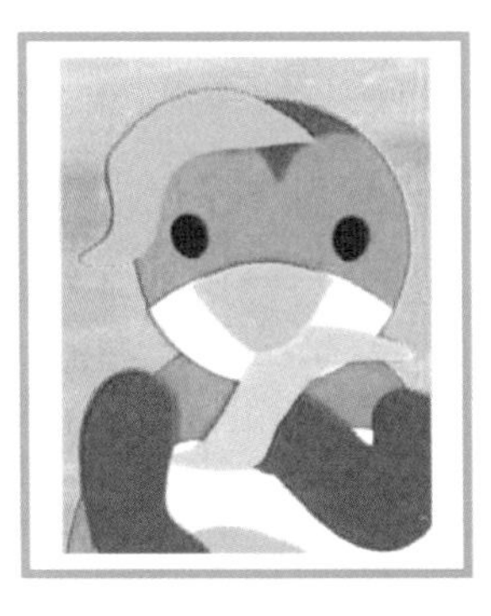

In her article, "Truth, Lies and Intimacy: An Attachment Perspective," Jude Cassidy outlines four traits associated with the capacity to participate in intimate relationships. These include the ability to give care, to receive care, to negotiate personal needs and to be our authentic self. These four traits are beautiful and mastering them is something we all strive to achieve.

One of the best ways to teach our children to be respectful is through modeling. Let's start with an inventory of how comfortable you as a parent are with the four traits. Ask yourself, on a 1-10 scale, 10 being the most comfortable, how comfortable are you...

Accepting help from others?

Giving help to others?

Being your authentic self?

Negotiating your own needs?

If you scored a low number on any of the four traits, you may have some reflective work of your own to do before you can properly model these core beliefs for your child. Often, adults who have difficulty trusting others will score lower on the 1-10 scale than adults comfortable with trust. This mistrust generally comes from early life experiences. Making sense of your own experiences and beliefs will help you model these traits for your children as well as provide you with a general sense of peace and understanding.

Accepting Help from Others:

Many of our foster and adopted children have had to meet their own needs as a way to survive. Some even cared for their younger siblings and assumed a parenting role. Children without a parent able to care for them likely did not learn to trust. Without trust, accepting help from others feels very uncomfortable and scary. A language of playfulness and safety is recommended when teaching your child to accept help. Statements such as these send a message of love and trust: "I love you very much. May I show you by tying your shoes for you?" or "While you go play and have fun, I will make the macaroni and cheese for you and your sister."

Giving Help to Others:

One way to show respect is to care for others when they have a need. Imagine your child offering a hand to the opposing teammate knocked down during a basketball game or holding the door open for another person. You would beam with pride! Helping others in need validates our belief that humans (and animals) are worthy of love and care. When you find yourself helping another person, point this out to your child and when you witness your children helping another, praise them.

Negotiating Needs:

Children from hard places were often on their own or were mistreated by adults who assumed power and control over them in hurtful ways. As a result, the ideas of shared power, choices and compromises are likely new to them. The first step in teaching this skill to our children is by negotiating with them ourselves. We give them a voice by offering compromises and sharing power. You can say something similar to, "It is time for snack. Would you like apples or bananas or another healthy snack as a compromise?" In this example both you and the child have their needs met.

The handout above was derived from Purvis, K.B., Cross, D.R. & Sunshine, W.L. (2007) *The Connected Child: Bringing Hope and Healing to Your Adoptive Family.* New York: McGraw-Hill and Cassidy, Jude. "Truth, Lies and Intimacy: An Attachment Perspective." *Attachment and Human Development, Vol 3 No2.* 2 September 2001: 121-155. Print.

How to Show Respect

Teaching Tips for Parents by Cindy R. Lee, LCSW

You ensure the child has a healthy snack and you shared power by allowing the child to choose the snack. In addition, playfully teaching them how to share with siblings and peers reinforces their ability to negotiate their own needs and the needs of others.

Being Your Authentic Self:

To be authentic we have to feel safe. To feel safe we have to be validated and given the opportunity to show our identity and creativity. Psychologists and therapists accomplish this with children by allowing opportunities for connecting through child-led play. As parents, our interactions with our children usually revolve around teaching, correcting, and questioning. Children explore being their authentic selves through play. Playing with them without leading allows you the opportunity to get to know them and to validate their unique ideas and creativity.

Teaching Respect:

How do we teach these four traits to our children and how do we help them believe that they and others are important and worthy of love? We provide children with opportunities to be authentic, we deeply connect with them so they learn trust, and we model our own beliefs through action.

To connect and allow the child an opportunity to be authentic, practice this child-led play exercise:

Child-Led Play Exercise

For a few minutes sit and play with your child without leading. Utilize a toy that allows for creativity. Play-Doh®, building blocks or white paper and crayons work very well. As you play, follow your child's lead by recreating what he or she builds or draws. Allow the ideas for play to be the child's ideas. Do what they want to do and validate their creative ideas and imaginative words. See if you can make it five minutes without taking away the lead. This exercise validates their authenticity and gives them confidence to be themselves!

To model your beliefs through action, work on being comfortable with the four traits. Your mastery will reflect in your actions and your children will model them. Be purposeful. The next time you write out that charitable gift check, show it to your children and explain why you are writing it.

To begin the conversation about these four traits, as well as teaching respectful behaviors, read *Penguin and the Fine-Looking Fish* to your child. You can process the book by asking your child the following questions:

- What disrespectful behaviors did the penguin show in the beginning?
- Penguin accepted the fish's help to pull the seaweed from the sea floor. Do you accept help from others?
- Penguin helped the fish by telling his family that he was safe. Do you offer to help others?
- How did Penguin and the fish negotiate their needs at the end of the story?
- Did Penguin show others his authentic self? In what way?

Once your child learns these traits, he or she will have an easier time showing respectful behavior. For example, when your child is sassy, you can say, "The way you are speaking does not show others respect. Please say that again with respect." When your child forgets to say "thank you," you can say, "How can we show respect when somebody gives us a gift?" Then your child will follow with a thank you. Using this model, children learn because they are given a reason why your request is appropriate, and they are given the chance to fix the behavior through action.

Have fun reading *The Penguin and the Fine-looking Fish* with your cuddle bugs.

For more great information, please read *The Connected Child* by Purvis, Cross and Lyons-Sunshine and visit www.empoweredtoconnect.org & www.tcu.child.edu.

The handout above was derived from Purvis, K.B., Cross, D.R. & Sunshine, W.L. (2007) *The Connected Child: Bringing Hope and Healing to Your Adoptive Family.* New York: McGraw-Hill and Cassidy, Jude. "Truth, Lies and Intimacy: An Attachment Perspective." *Attachment and Human Development, Vol 3 No2.* 2 September 2001: 121-155. Print.

Penguin was separated from the people, places and family he was familiar with.

When this happened,

his kind and gentle heart

filled with fear.

He protected himself from danger by
looking up and down
and all around.

He struggled to focus and flipped his flippers
to manage the fear he felt.

Because he felt so alone, he didn't know how to act.

He no longer accepted help, he no longer gave help and he no longer showed respect to himself and others.

When he saw some food, he took it.

If he was told to share, he wouldn't.

If he was asked to help, he couldn't.

Penguin spoke sassy, ate sloppy and forgot to say please.

Penguin's new family and friends did not understand his hurting heart.

His desire to feel safe led him in search of a pet that would love him and never leave him.

Penguin found the most
fantastic, fascinating, fine-looking fish
he had ever fixed his eyes on.

"I will catch it and care for it and call it my friend," he thought to himself.

Penguin caught the fish and kept it safe and sound.

Each morning he swam to the fish,

served it seaweed

and kept it company.

One day Penguin had a problem pulling the seaweed from the sea floor.

“Let me help you,” offered the fish.

“I am too afraid to accept help,” Penguin softly sighed.

Although he tried, Penguin was not strong enough to pull the seaweed by himself.

"Let me help you."

"All will be aaaalllright,"

promised the fish.

Penguin finally accepted the fish's help but forgot to say thank you.

“Remember kind Penguin, accepting help and saying thank you are respectful actions,” encouraged the fish.

The next day the fish asked,

"Could you please inform my family that I am safe and sound?"

"I am too afraid to help others," admitted Penguin.

"All will be aaaalllright,"

promised the fish.

So Penguin told the fish's family that the fish was safe and sound.

The family thanked him and gave him some advice.

"Remember gentle Penguin, one way to show respect is to offer help to others."

When Penguin returned, the fish inquired,
"Tell me about yourself."

"Well, I used to be kind, quick and creative, and I could find more food than any penguin in the cool blue sea!"

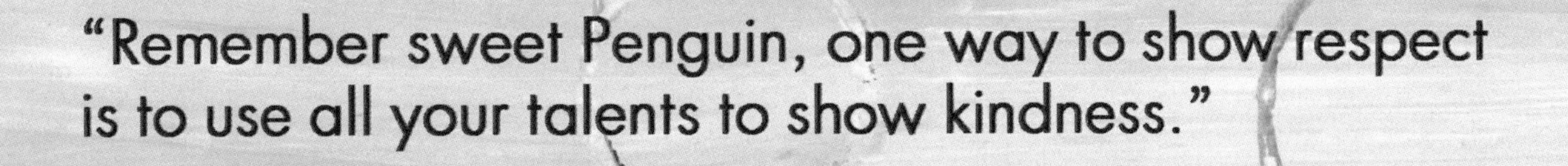

“Remember sweet Penguin, one way to show respect is to use all your talents to show kindness.”

“All will be aaaalllright,”

promised the fish.

Feeling safe and loved, Penguin hurried home to show his new family his respectful actions.

He helped others by using his super-fast swimming skills to snag seaweed for supper.

He accepted help from his Nana who showed him how to use a napkin so he could stay neat.

He even said, "Please!"

His proud parents praised him for being so respectful.

That evening, Penguin thanked the fine-looking fish.

“Thank you for loving me and helping me feel safe.
How can I show you love in return?”

The fish replied,

“You have taken good care of me,

but it is time for me to be with my family.”

“But you are my only friend.
Due to my disrespectful actions,
the penguins do not want to play with me.”

“I know a way that I can be with my family and you can find friends,” suggested the fish.

"You accept help from others,

give help to others,

and act kind and gentle."

"If you show your penguin peers these friendly features they will easily become your penguin pals."

Penguin could not argue with the wisdom of the fish.

He gave the fish a see-you-later smile
and sent him on his way.

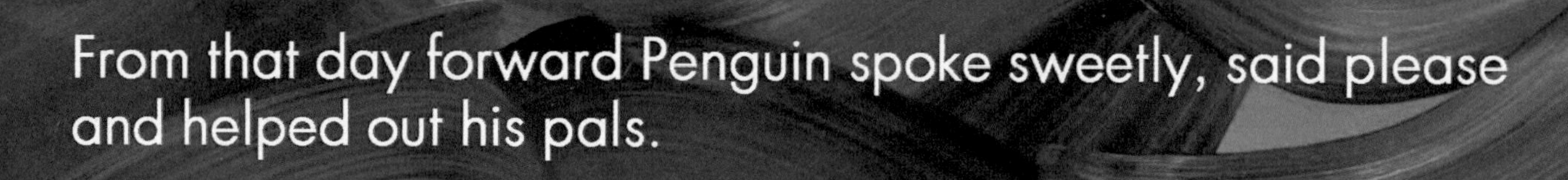

From that day forward Penguin spoke sweetly, said please and helped out his pals.

His new friends and family met all his needs and Penguin felt safe.

The kind, respectful penguin and the fine-looking fish played together every day.

They stayed forever friends and filled each other's hearts with love.

“All is aaaalllright!”

About the Author:

Cindy R. Lee is a Licensed Clinical Social Worker and Licensed Drug and Alcohol Counselor in private practice. Cindy is the co-founder and Executive Director of HALO Project, which is an intensive outpatient program for foster and adopt children and their families. Cindy resides in Edmond, Oklahoma with her husband, children and pets.

The Penguin and the Fine-Looking Fish is one of eight children's books designed to teach Trust Based Relational Intervention (TBRI) principles. TBRI was developed by Dr. Karyn Purvis and Dr. David Cross from TCU's Institute of Child Development. For more information, please visit www.child.tcu.edu.

Made in the USA
Lexington, KY
05 September 2019